AUSSIE BIG ACHIEVERS

ASH BARTY

written by RICHARD SIMPKIN

illustrated by DEBRA O'HALLORAN

Other AUSSIE BIG ACHIEVERS books
STEVE IRWIN
CATHY FREEMAN
SHANE WARNE

We acknowledge the Traditional Owners of the land on which we publish books, the Quandamooka people and pay our respects to Elders past, present and emerging.

Published by:
Boolarong Press,
38/1631 Wynnum Road
Tingalpa Qld 4173
Australia.
www.boolarongpress.com.au

First published 2021

A catalogue record for this book is available from the National Library of Australia

ISBN: 9781922643186 (Paperback)

Printed and bound by Watson Ferguson & Company, Tingalpa, Australia

DEDICATION

This book is dedicated to You,
because You can achieve any dream You have!

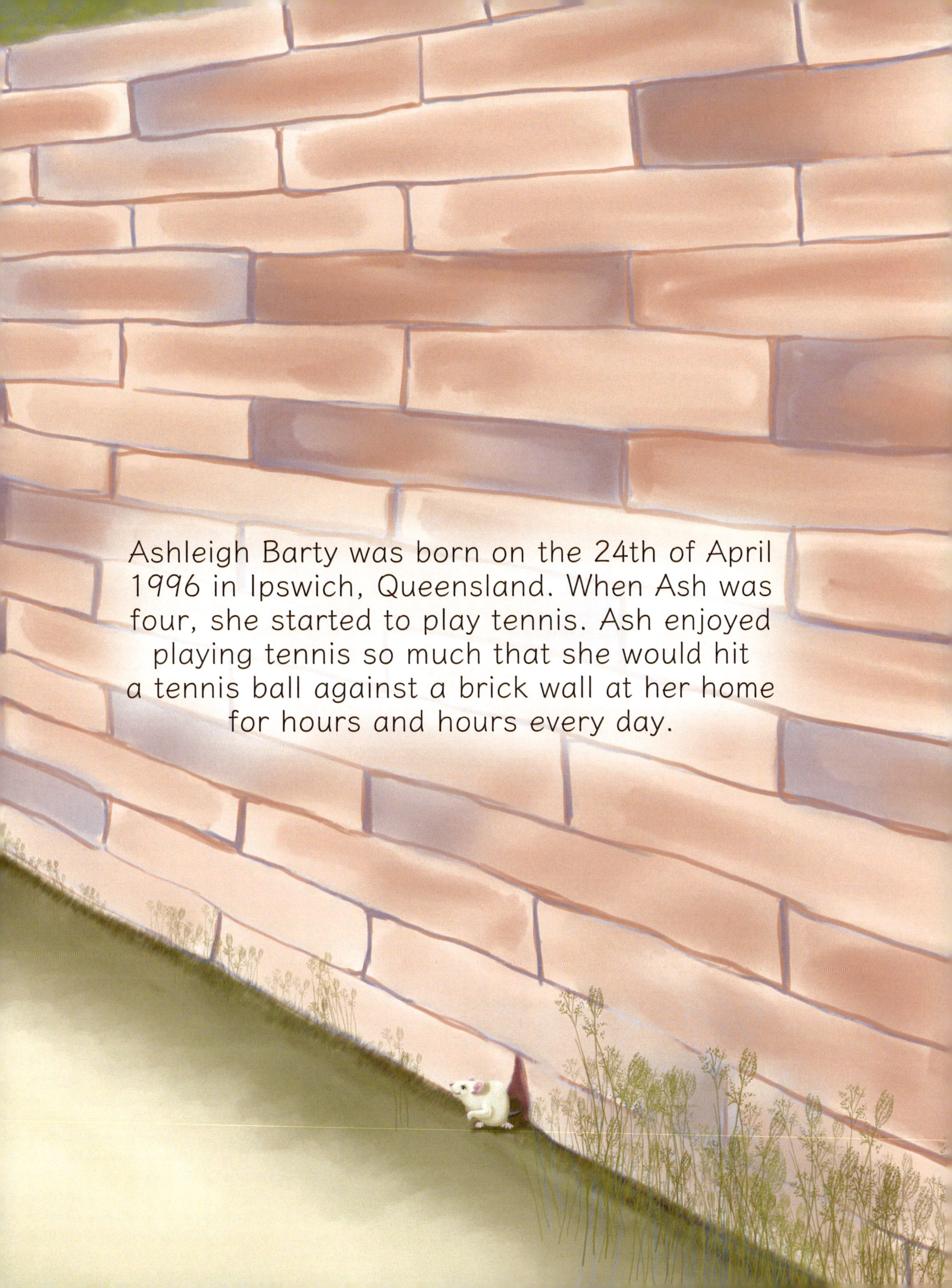

Ashleigh Barty was born on the 24th of April 1996 in Ipswich, Queensland. When Ash was four, she started to play tennis. Ash enjoyed playing tennis so much that she would hit a tennis ball against a brick wall at her home for hours and hours every day.

Ash's parents realised that she really loved playing tennis, so they decided to meet with Jim Joyce who was a tennis coach. Jim hit the ball over to Ash and bang! Ash hit the ball back to him with almost lightning speed. Jim could see she already had incredible talent with a high level of focus.

With guidance from her parents and coach, Ash started entering tennis tournaments. She was so good that she used to practise against adults, and guess what? She was beating a lot of them!

When Ash was twelve, she found out that her great-grandmother was part of the Ngaragu people and Ash felt very proud that she was an Aboriginal Australian. Ash's dream was to one day win Wimbledon. Her idol was Evonne Goolagong-Cawley who is also Aboriginal. Evonne won Wimbledon in 1971 and again in 1980. Ash wanted to be just like Evonne.

Ash believed in herself and dreamed of one day becoming the best tennis player in the world. She started playing tennis tournaments all around the world. When Ash was fifteen, she won the 2011 Wimbledon Junior Championships. She was also named tennis junior athlete of the year.

In 2013, Ash partnered with fellow Australian Cassey Dellacqua and in January of that year, Ash and Cassey made the doubles final of the Australian Open. Ash was still only sixteen. Ash and Cassey went on to reach two more Grand Slam women's finals that year at Wimbledon and the US Open.

In 2014 when Ash was 18, she decided that she needed a break from tennis. Ash wanted to play a team sport so decided to play cricket. In 2015 Ash signed with the Brisbane Heat in the Women's Big Bash League. In her first game she made 39 runs off just 27 balls; she even scored a six! Ash proved that if you have a dream and believe in yourself then you can achieve anything.

After a season of playing cricket, Ash returned to tennis with great enthusiasm and started playing tournaments again. At the US Open in 2018, Ash and her partner, CoCo Vandeweghe, got through to the doubles finals after beating the number one seeds. After they lost the first set, Ash and her partner won the next two sets to win the US Open Doubles finals to claim her first Grand Slam title.

In 2019, Ash won the Miami Open after beating three of the top ten players in the world. Ash was playing extremely well and entered the French Open full of confidence. During the two-week tournament, Ash only lost two sets and ended up winning the French Open. Ash was now a Grand Slam singles champion.

After winning the French Open, Ash then won the Birmingham Classic and in doing so she became the world's number one women's tennis player. This was an incredible achievement, as just two and a half years earlier she was ranked 272 in the world. Ash's hard work, self-belief and never giving up attitude showed us all that anything is possible; you just have to believe in yourself.

In January 2020, Ash was named Young Australian of The Year. Ash decided not to play in tournaments around the world, but continued to practise for the 2021 season. It had been ten years since Ash won the 2011 Wimbledon Junior Championships; could Ash go one step further and win the Ladies Single's Wimbledon Championships?

Ash entered Wimbledon 2021 as world number one. After winning the first round in three sets, Ash then won the next five matches without dropping a single set to go through to the Ladies' final. As a tribute to Evonne, Ash wore a similar tennis outfit to what Evonne wore fifty years earlier when she won Wimbledon. If there was ever a time when Ash needed to believe in herself it was now.

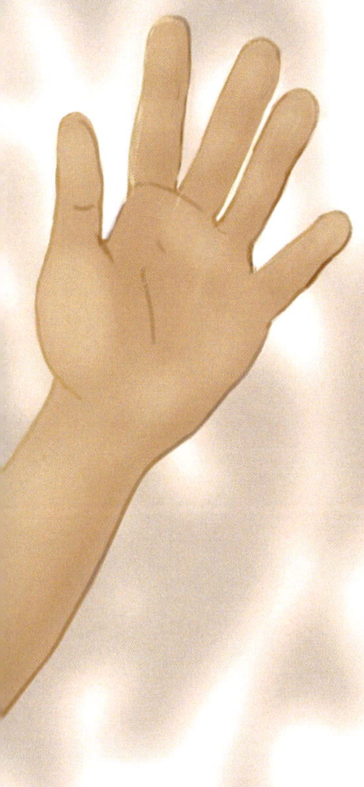

On the 10th of July 2021, Ash walked onto the centre court of Wimbledon to a sellout crowd of 15,000 fans. Ash had dreamed of this moment for most of her life. All of Australia were shouting with excitement: Go Ash Go!

Ash won the first set, but then lost the second in a tie-break. The 15,000 fans in the stadium including The Duchess of Cambridge and Prince William were all on the edge of their seats. Ash started the third set well and eventually won the set 6-3. Ash had done it; she had won Wimbledon! The whole of Australia jumped out of their seats with excitement; it was time for a "Barty Party".

Ash had achieved her lifelong dream of winning Wimbledon and by doing so she inspired kids from Australia and all around the world to follow their dreams.

Ash's next big dream was to win the 2022 Australian Open which is held every year in Melbourne Australia.

In January 2022 the Australian Open was held and Ash went into the tournament as the world's number one female tennis player. It had been forty-four years since an Australian had won the women's singles title.

Ash had the weight of the nation on her shoulders. Could Ash win the Australian Open in her home country?

For the next two weeks Ash believed in herself and won every single match without dropping a single set to reach the finals.

On the 29th of January Ash entered the Rod Laver arena to thousands of fans yelling, go Ash go!

Ash won the first set six games to three, but in the second set she was down five games to one.

Ash had to stay focused and believe that she could win. Incredibly Ash eventually won the second set seven games to six in a tie-break and by doing so she won the 2022 Australian Open.

Ash achieved another one of her dreams and in doing so she inspired children to pick up a tennis racket and believe in themselves; because if you do, then one day you too can be a champion just like Ash Barty.

FUN QUESTIONS

[1] How old was Ash when she first started playing tennis?

[2] What did Ash find out when she was twelve?

[3] What was Ash's dream?

[4] Who is Ash's idol?

[5] How old was Ash when she won the 2011 Wimbledon Junior Championships?

[6] Besides tennis, what other sport did Ash play?

[7] What year was Ash named Young Australian of The Year?

[8] What was Ash ranked during Wimbledon 2021?

[9] Who won the Ladies Singles Wimbledon Championships in 2021?

[10] How many sets did Ash lose during the entire Australian Open 2022?

ABOUT THE AUTHOR

Richard Simpkin was born in Sydney, Australia in 1973 and has worked as a photographer in Australia, England and the US for 25 years.

He is a best-selling author of five books, two of which are about Australian legends who he met, photographed and interviewed.

In 2014 Richard also founded World Letter Writing Day and has inspired children and adults all around the world to take a break from social media and write handwritten letters.

Richard has also conducted many workshops at schools in Australia. The students often ask him about many of the Australian legends that he has met over the years. This has inspired Richard to create these fun yet educational books about iconic Australians who we should all know about.

Other books by author

Australian Legends, 2005
Richard and Famous, 2007
100 Australian Legends, 2014
Michael in Pictures, 2015
Richard Simpkin Celebrity Quotes, 2016
Steve Irwin — Aussie Big Achievers, 2021
Cathy Freeman — Aussie Big Achievers, 2021
Shane Warne — Aussie Big Achievers, 2022

OTHER AUSSIE BIG ACHIEVERS BOOKS